Superphonics … to learn to read using … ective phonic m…od. … story is fun to read … as been carefu… …tten to include particular sounds and spellings.

The Storybooks are graded so your child can progress with confidence from easy words to harder ones. There are four levels - Blue (the easiest), Green, Purple and Turquoise (the hardest). Each level is linked to one of the core *Superphonics*® *Books*.

ISBN-13: 978 0 340 77353 6

Editorial by Gill Munton
Design by Sarah Borny

First published in Great Britain 2002

10 9 8 7 6 5 4

First published in 2002 by Hodder Children's Books, a division of Hachette Children's Books, 338 Euston Road, London NW1 3BH

Printed in China by WKT Company Ltd

A CIP record is registered by and held at the British Library.

Target words

All the Blue Storybooks focus on the following sounds:

a as in **sat**
i as in **did**
u as in **dug**
e as in **bed**
o as in **hop**

These target words are featured in the book:

at	bed	big	Dot	but
bad	Ed	did	got	cut
Max	get	Fig	Hob	dug
ran	legs	hid	hog	put
sat	them	him	hop	tum
	then	in	not	up
	yes	pit	on	
		sit	top	
		thin		

Other words

Also included are some common words (e.g. **and**, **was**) which your child will be learning in his or her first few years at school.

A few other words have been used to help the stories to flow.

Reading the book

1 Make sure you and your child are sitting in a quiet, comfortable place.

2 Tell him or her a little about the stories, without giving too much away:

In the first story, some animal friends try their best to get a lazy dinosaur out of bed.

In the second story, a huntsman is not as brave as he thought he was!

This will give your child a mental picture; having a context for a story makes it easier to read the words.

3 Read the target words (above) together. This will mean that you can both enjoy the stories without having to spend too much time working out the words. Help your child to sound out each word (e.g. **b**-**e**-**d**) before saying the whole word.

4 Let your child read each of the stories aloud. Help him or her with any difficult words and discuss the story as you go along. Stop now and again to ask your child to predict what will happen next. This will help you to see whether he or she has understood what has happened so far.

Above all, enjoy the stories, and praise your child's reading!

4

Ruth Miskin's

Superphonics®

Blue Storybook

Get Up!

by Gill Munton

Illustrated by Kate Sheppard

a division of Hachette Children's Books

Get up!

Dot was in bed.

“Get up!” said Max.
“Get up, or I will
tickle your tum!”

But Dot did not get up.

“Get up!” said Hob.
“Get up, or I will
get into your bed!”

But Dot did not get up.

"Get up!" said Fig.
"Get up, or I will
hop up and down
on your legs!"

But Dot did not get up.

"Get up!" said Ed.
"Get up, or I will
sit on you!"

But Dot did not get up.

So Max tickled her tum ...

... and Hob
got into her bed ...

... and Fig
hopped up and down
on her legs ...

... and Ed sat on her.

"Get up!" they said.

Dot looked at Max,
and Hob, and Fig,
and Ed.

"I can't get up!"
she said.

I went to hunt
the Big Bad Hog!

Did you?

Yes!

I dug a pit.

Did you?

Yes!

Then I cut some thin sticks,
and put them on top.

Did you?

Yes!

And when
the Big Bad Hog came,
I got a big stick,
and I ran up to him ...

Did you?

No.

I just hid!